Charles Dickens'

A Christmas Carol

For Iggy, with love

First published 2002 in *Charles Dickens and Friends*
by Walker Books Ltd, 87 Vauxhall Walk, London SE11 5HJ

This edition published 2014

1 3 5 7 9 10 8 6 4 2

© Marcia Williams 2014, 2007, 2002

The right of Marcia Williams to be identified as author/illustrator of this work
has been asserted by her in accordance with the Copyright, Designs and Patents Act 1988

This book has been typeset in Kennerly Regular

Printed and bound in Great Britain by Clays Ltd, St Ives plc

British Library Cataloguing in Publication Data:
a catalogue record for this book is available from the British Library

ISBN 978-1-4063-5694-6

Charles Dickens'

A Christmas Carol

Retold and Illustrated by

Marcia Williams

WALKER BOOKS

AND SUBSIDIARIES

LONDON · BOSTON · SYDNEY · AUCKLAND

Contents

Chapter One
Christmas Eve

Everyone knew old Ebenezer Scrooge was
the most tight-fisted miser you could meet.
Yes, Ebenezer Scrooge was as hard as flint.
A squeezing, wrenching, grasping, scraping,
clutching, covetous old sinner! The cold
within him froze his old features and made
his eyes red and his thin lips blue. Nobody
ever stopped Scrooge in the street to say,

"My dear Scrooge, how are you?" No beggars asked him for a penny, no children asked him what time it was. Even the blind man's dog dragged his master away from Scrooge. Yet what did Scrooge care? It was just how he liked it. He was as solitary as an oyster.

Scrooge ran a counting-house and had once had a business partner, Jacob Marley,

who had also been a tight-fisted miser.
Jacob had been dead for seven years.
There was no doubt that he was dead.
No doubt at all, and this must be clearly
understood, or the story I am about to
relate will hold no wonder. In life, Scrooge
had been Marley's only friend and his
only mourner in death. There could be

no doubt about it – Scrooge knew for certain that Jacob Marley was dead!

On a freezing Christmas Eve, Scrooge sat in his cold office counting the coals Bob Cratchit, his clerk, put on the fire. He grumbled that Christmas was all "humbug".

Scrooge carried ice within his heart and it didn't thaw one single degree at Christmas-time, not even when his cheerful nephew, Fred, burst through the door.

"A Merry Christmas, Uncle!" he cried. "Come, dine with us tomorrow."

"Bah!" said Scrooge. "Humbug!"

"Christmas a humbug, Uncle?" said Fred. "You don't mean that, I'm sure?"

Scrooge crossly refused Fred's invitation

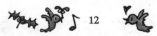

and saw him to the door without so
much as a "Merry Christmas!"

When two portly gentlemen came
collecting money to buy meat, drink
and coal for the poor, Scrooge sent
them away empty-handed.

"Are there no prisons? No workhouses?"
he demanded crossly.

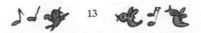

"There are, but many can't go there; and many would rather die first," replied the gentlemen.

"Well, if those that are badly off choose not to go to the prisons and workhouses, they had better die and decrease the surplus population! I don't make merry myself at Christmas and I can't afford to make idle people merry."

14

Meanwhile the fog thickened, darkness fell and lanterns were held high. Teeth chattered and limbs shivered as the chill became more intense. A little boy, as thin and cold as the bones gnawed by a dog, bent to sing a carol through Scrooge's keyhole: "God bless you, merry gentlemen! May nothing you dismay!"

"Bah, humbug!" shouted Scrooge, taking a ruler and shaking it at the singer with such

energy that he fled in terror.

At length it was time to shut the counting-house for the day. Scrooge turned to poor Bob Cratchit. "You'll want all day off tomorrow, I suppose?" he said.

"If quite convenient, sir," replied Bob.

"It's not convenient," said Scrooge, "and it's not fair. I should stop your wages for it."

It was a cold and bitter night before Scrooge let Bob go home. He did not wish him a Merry Christmas, just warned him

that he had better make up the lost hours
by coming in all the earlier the morning
after Christmas.

You will not be surprised to hear that
Scrooge's melancholy tavern meal that night
was meagre with only his banker's book
for company. Nor will it surprise you that
the lodgings he made his way to afterwards
were bleak and lonely.

Chapter Two
Marley's Ghost

What it may surprise you to learn is
what Scrooge saw when he reached
his lodgings. Jacob Marley's face was in
the door knocker! It was not angry or
ferocious, but looked at Scrooge as
Marley used to look. It was not just
the shadow of a face, but as clear and
as livid in colour as a bad lobster. It was

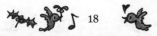

horrible to behold, and to say that Scrooge
was not startled would be untrue – yet
ignoring it, he turned his key resolutely
in the lock, walked into his gloomy hallway
and lit a candle.

"Pooh, pooh!" he said to the knocker and
slammed the front door shut.

Scrooge went to make some gruel upon
his meagre fire, but there in every fireplace
tile was Marley's face looking out at him!

"Humbug!" said Scrooge as he walked away.

After several turns around the room he sat down again, but then all the clock bells in the room began to ring at once and a chain clanked upon the stair.

"It's humbug still!" said Scrooge. "I won't believe it."

But Scrooge turned pale when Marley himself floated through the door! Still he would not believe it, and told the ghost he

was the product of indigestion.

"You may be an undigested bit of beef," he protested, "a blot of mustard, or a fragment of potato. There's more of gravy than of grave about you."

At this, the ghost untied the bandage around his head and as his jaw fell to his chest, a fearful wail came out of it. Scrooge fell quaking to his knees.

"Mercy, dreadful apparition, why do you trouble me?" he asked.

"I come to warn you," wailed Marley's ghost. "I did not go forth to help in the world during my life, so now my spirit is condemned to do so. I wear the chain I forged in life. I made it link by link, and yard by yard."

Marley told Scrooge the chain of keys and cash boxes he wore was the result of his miserly life. He begged Scrooge to change his ways before he died, or he would become a fettered phantom too!

"Jacob," implored Scrooge. "Speak comfort to me."

"You will be visited by three spirits," Marley told Scrooge. "Expect the first tomorrow, when the bell tolls one; the

second on the next night at the same hour;
and the third on the next night on the last
stroke of twelve."

He begged Scrooge to learn from them.
"Without their visits," said Marley, "you
cannot hope to shun the path I tread."

Then, as Scrooge stared in horror, the
spectre bound its head again, took up its
chain and walked towards the window.
As the window opened itself, old Marley's
ghost floated backwards out of it.

"Remember what has passed between
us!" cried Marley.

The night air he joined was thick with moaning phantoms. Each wore a heavy chain. Still in his dressing gown, Scrooge fell into bed. He tried to say "humbug", but couldn't. "Hum ... hum ... hu..." was all he could manage.

Chapter Three
The Ghost of Christmas Past

Scrooge slept fitfully. When he awoke the clock was chiming the hour of one o'clock. A light flashed in the room and the curtains of his bed parted. Scrooge found himself face to face with another unearthly visitor. It had the face and body of a child, but long grey hair and muscular arms, and there was

a jet of light shining out from the top of its head. It held a branch of fresh green holly in its hand and under its arm it held its hat – a giant candle snuffer.

"I am the Ghost of Christmas Past," said the Ghost in a soft and gentle voice.

"Long past?" inquired Scrooge.

"No. Your past," it answered. "Rise and walk with me!"

Scrooge rose, but when the Ghost made

towards the window, Scrooge grabbed for
its robe.

"I am a mortal," he said, "and liable to fall."

Gently, the Ghost took Scrooge by the
arm and guided him through his bedroom
wall and back through the years.

First, they came to a classroom
where a lonely boy sat reading. Scrooge
recognized his boy-self, left in school
over the Christmas holiday by his
unloving father.

"Poor boy!" said Scrooge, in pity for his former self.

"Your lip is trembling," said the Ghost, "and what is that upon your cheek?"

Scrooge brushed aside a tear, muttering that it was a pimple.

Next, Scrooge saw a later Christmas. His kind sister, Fan – who was now dead – had come to take him home.

"I have come to bring you home, dear

brother," she said. "Home, home,
home!"

Remembering Fan, Scrooge realised
that it was only today that he had refused
her son's welcoming invitation to share
Christmas dinner with his family.

"Fan was always a delicate creature," said
the Ghost. "But she had a large heart!"

"So she had," cried Scrooge, beginning
to feel mean.

Next, the Ghost took them to a
merry Christmas party at the first
office Scrooge had worked in. Mr Fezziwig,
his employer, had been a generous old
gentleman. A fire blazed, candles shone
and there was food, a fiddler, wine and
laughter. Scrooge watched his young self
and his companions making merry. He
thought of his own clerk, poor, cold
Bob Cratchit. Scrooge saw that – like
Fezziwig – he had the power to render

Bob happy or unhappy.

"I should like to be able to say a word or two to my clerk just now!" said Scrooge.

"My time grows short," observed the Ghost. "Quick!"

The scene changed and again Scrooge saw himself. He was older, a man in the prime of life. His face didn't have the hard, rigid lines it bore now, but it had begun to show the signs of greed. He was not alone, and sitting beside the younger Ebenezer

Scrooge was the woman he had hoped to
marry. She had watched Ebenezer's love
for her fade, as his passion for money grew.
Sadly she had broken their engagement.

"The master-passion, Gain, engrosses
you," she said softly. "May you be happy
in the life you have chosen!" She left him
and they parted.

"Spirit!" said Scrooge. "Show me no
more! Conduct me home. Why do you
delight to torture me?"

Scrooge couldn't bear
it any longer. He seized
the Ghost's hat, snuffed out
its light, fell into bed and slept.

Chapter Four
The Ghost of Christmas Present

Scrooge woke the next night in the middle of a prodigiously loud snore! The clock struck one o'clock and Scrooge saw that the next room was ablaze with light. Shuffling to the door, he saw that the walls were covered with holly, mistletoe and ivy. The floor was piled with food: turkeys, geese, sausages, red-hot chestnuts, cake,

pears, oranges and great bowls of punch.
In the middle of this sumptuous feast sat
a jolly giant.

"Come in," exclaimed the Ghost. "I am
the Ghost of Christmas Present. Come in
and know me better, man!"

"Spirit," said Scrooge. "Conduct me where
you will. If you have aught to teach me, let
me profit by it."

"Touch my robe!" the Ghost replied.

Scrooge did as he was told and the Ghost

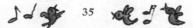

rose. Holding up a horn of light, it transported Scrooge out into the streets of Christmas morning.

They came to Bob Cratchit's cramped little home. It was a bustle of Christmas preparations. Bob had just come in from church with his frail son, Tiny Tim, on his shoulders.

"God bless us, every one!" said Tiny Tim.

Bob lowered him onto a stool and sat

himself close to the child. He held Tiny Tim's withered little hand in his, as if to keep the child with him forever.

When Mrs Cratchit served a small but sizzling pudding, all the children cheered. But when Bob proposed a toast to his employer, they all fell silent.

Next they came to Scrooge's nephew Fred's house. Fred was making his whole family laugh by telling stories of his miserly uncle.

"He said that Christmas was humbug, as I live!" he cried. "He believed it too! He's a comical fellow and that's the truth: and not so pleasant as he might be."

After tea, Fred's family had some music and singing and then all the adults played games with the children. Scrooge was so drawn in by their merriment that he began to feel a part of it, but the Ghost would not let him stay.

Lastly, the Ghost showed Scrooge a vision: two wretched, ragged children, born of human selfishness and greed.

"Spirit!" asked Scrooge. "Are they yours?"

"They are Man's..." the Ghost replied. "The boy is Ignorance. The girl is Want. Beware of them both."

"Have they no refuge or money?" cried Scrooge.

"Are there no prisons, no workhouses?" said the Ghost, turning on him with Scrooge's own words.

The clock struck again. The Ghost vanished.

Chapter Five
The Ghost of Christmas Yet to Come

The following night, as the sound of
the final chime of twelve o'clock faded,
Scrooge looked about him and as he did
so, a silent and hooded ghost drifted like
mist towards him. It was shrouded in a
deep black garment, which concealed all
save one outstretched hand. Its mysterious
presence filled Scrooge with dread.

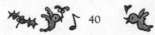

"I am in the presence of the Ghost of Christmas Yet To Come?" asked Scrooge. "I fear you more than any spectre."

The Ghost gave no reply. The hand pointed straight before them.

"Lead on!" said Scrooge, though his legs trembled beneath him so that he could hardly stand.

The Ghost moved away and Scrooge followed in the shadow of its robe, which bore him up and carried him along.

Scrooge was transported to the city district where he worked. Some businessmen known to Scrooge were laughing over a recent death.

"It's likely to be a very cheap funeral," said one. "I don't know of anybody to go to it."

"Wicked old screw, wasn't he?" said another.

The Ghost glided on down a dingy alley where two women were selling the same dead man's possessions for profit.

"What odds?" said one of the women. "Every person has a right to take care of themselves. He always did."

"He was a mean, tight-fisted old devil," said her companion. "If he'd been more natural in his lifetime he'd have had someone to care for him, instead of lying there gasping out his last, alone by himself."

"Am I that man?" asked Scrooge.

The Ghost did not reply, but moved on

to where a young family were rejoicing at
the man's death. They owed him money
that they could not afford to pay back

Scrooge felt sorry for the unmourned man
and asked the Ghost to show him the death
of someone who was loved. The Ghost took
him to the Cratchits' home. Bob had just
returned from visiting a new grave, dug for

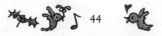

Tiny Tim. The family grew closer
together, remembering the gentle boy
they would miss so much.

"My little, little child," cried Bob.

"Don't mind it, Father," said his
youngest daughter.

"I am sure we shall none of us forget
poor Tiny Tim, shall we?" said Bob.

"Never, Father!" the child replied.

"No, Spirit! Oh, no, no!" cried Scrooge.

He asked the name of the friendless man again. This time, the Ghost took him to a churchyard. There, on a neglected grave, Scrooge read his own name. Scrooge clutched the Ghost's hand.

"Oh, tell me I may sponge away the writing on this stone!"

The Ghost's hand trembled.

"Assure me that I yet may change these

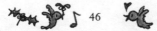

shadows you have shown me, by an altered life. I will honour Christmas in my heart, and try to keep it all the year. I will live in the Past, Present and Future!"

The Ghost answered not a word, but disappeared back into Scrooge's bedpost.

Chapter Six
The End of It

Scrooge checked the bedpost. Yes, it was his own. The bed was his own, he was back in his own bedroom and it was Christmas morning!

"Oh Jacob Marley, thank you and the spirits all for this chance to make amends!" he cheered.

Scrooge was so flustered and so glowing

with good intentions that he found himself
unable to put his clothes on in their proper
order. Garments turned inside out and
upside down, got lost and joined together
in the most wild and extravagant manner.

"I don't know what to do!" cried Scrooge,
laughing and crying in the same breath and
making a perfect muddle of his stockings.
"I am as happy as an angel! I am as merry
as a schoolboy! I am as giddy as a drunken

man! A merry Christmas to everybody!
A happy New Year to all the world.
Whoop! Hallo!"

For a man who had not practised jollity
for so many years, it was a splendid
performance! Running to the window,
Scrooge threw it open and stuck out
his head.

"What's today?" shouted Scrooge,
to a boy in his Sunday clothes.

"Today?" returned the boy with wonder. "Why, Christmas Day!"

Laughing with joy that he hadn't missed Christmas, he sent the boy running to fetch the prize turkey from the poultry shop for the Cratchits.

"Not the little prize turkey, mind," said Scrooge, "The big one!"

"What, the one as big as me?" returned the boy.

"Come back with it in five minutes," cried Scrooge, "and I'll give you half-a-crown."

"I'll send it to Bob Cratchit's!" he whispered, rubbing his hands and laughing.

Scrooge finished dressing as best he could and went out into the streets. As he pulled his front door shut, the knocker that had so recently held Jacob Marley's face caught his eye.

"I shall love it, as long as I live!" said
Scrooge, patting the knocker with his hand.

"And here's the turkey!" exclaimed Scrooge.
"Why, it's impossible to carry that. You must
have a cab."

At last, Scrooge set out into the streets.
Filled with Christmas cheer, he regarded
everyone with a delighted smile. He looked
so pleasant that people said, "Good morning,

sir! A merry Christmas to you!" How great these greetings sounded to Scrooge.

He had not gone far when he saw one of the two gentlemen who'd come collecting for the poor. Scrooge grabbed the man by the hands and donated a huge sum of money.

"My dear Mr Scrooge, are you serious?"

"If you please," said Scrooge. "Not a farthing less. A great many back-payments are included in it, I assure you."

Then Scrooge went to church.
Afterwards he walked about the streets,
watching the people hurrying by and
patting children on the head. He chatted
to beggars, looked into windows and
found that everything gave him the
greatest pleasure.

In the afternoon he turned his steps
towards his nephew's house. He passed the
door a dozen times before he plucked up the

courage to knock. In the end he made a dash and went for it!

"Will you let me in, Fred?" said Scrooge.

"Why bless my soul, it's Uncle Scrooge, so it is!" replied Fred.

It was a mercy Fred didn't shake Scrooge's arm off, such was his delight at seeing his uncle. Scrooge felt at home in five minutes. It was the merriest Christmas party. Wonderful games, wonderful music, wonderful friendship and wonderful happiness.

The next morning Scrooge was at his office early. He had set his heart on catching Bob arriving late – and so he did, a full eighteen minutes and a half late! His hat was off before he entered

the door and he was on his stool in a jiffy, but there was no doubt that he was late.

"I am not going to stand for this," said Scrooge.

Bob's heart sank.

"Therefore," continued Scrooge, "I am going to raise your salary, and endeavour to assist your struggling family. Now, go and buy another coal-scuttle before you dot another 'i', Bob Cratchit!"

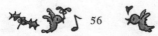

Bob could hardly believe his ears. He was not going to lose his job for being late or have his pay docked – he was going to receive a salary rise!

"A merry Christmas, Bob!" smiled Scrooge. "A merrier Christmas, my good fellow, than I have given you for many a year!"

From that day on, Scrooge proved the kindest, merriest old gentleman you could ever wish to meet. He was a friend to all, and to Tiny Tim – who did not die – he was a second father. When people laughed at the sudden change in him, he let them.

Scrooge never saw a ghost again, but he thanked old Marley from the bottom

of his heart for the lessons he had learnt.
Never again was he called a "wicked old
screw". Instead, it was always said of him
that he knew how to keep Christmas well.

May that be truly said of each of us.

Merry Christmas, everyone!

THE END

Charles Dickens

Charles Dickens was a respected novelist who lived in Victorian England. He went to various schools until he started work aged fifteen – although he spent an unhappy period labouring in a factory when he was twelve. He wrote fourteen novels and many other shorter stories, becoming the most famous writer of the time. He died in 1870.

Marcia Williams

Marcia Williams' mother was a novelist and her father a playwright, so it's not surprising that Marcia ended up an author herself. Her distinctive comic-strip style goes back to her schooldays in Sussex and the illustrated letters she sent home to her parents overseas.

Although she never trained formally as an artist, she found that motherhood, and the time she spent later as a nursery school teacher, inspired her to start writing and illustrating children's books.

Marcia's books bring to life some of the world's all-time favourite stories and some colourful historical characters. Her hilarious retellings and clever observations will have children laughing out loud and coming back for more!

Books in this series

ISBN 978-1-4063-5692-2

ISBN 978-1-4063-5695-3

ISBN 978-1-4063-5693-9

ISBN 978-1-4063-5694-6

Available from all good booksellers

www.walker.co.uk